MORE
THAN
PSALMS

ANTHEMS FROM THE PSALMS
FOR MIXED VOICE CHOIRS

SELECTED AND EDITED BY BARRY ROSE

NOVELLO

LONDON

FRONT COVER photograph of Wells Cathedral Choristers and
Lay Vicars by Tony Bolton
BACK COVER photograph of Barry Rose by Timothy Hands

COVER DESIGN Miranda Harvey

MUSIC SETTING Stave Origination

NOV040062
ISBN 0-7119-9774-8

© Copyright 2003 Novello & Company Ltd.
Published in Great Britain by Novello Publishing Limited.

HEAD OFFICE
8/9 Frith Street,
London W1D 3JB
England
Tel +44 (0)20 7434 0066
Fax +44 (0)20 7287 6329

SALES AND HIRE
Music Sales Limited,
Newmarket Road,
Bury St Edmunds,
Suffolk IP33 3YB
England
Tel +44 (0)1284 702600
Fax +44 (0)1284 768301

www.chesternovello.com
e-mail: music@musicsales.co.uk

Other anthologies by Barry Rose available from Novello:

High Praise NOV032118
Merrily on High NOV032121
More than Hymns 1 NOV040043
More than Hymns 2 NOV040044
Sing Low NOV381000

Contents

Preface

Across the centuries, composers have often turned to the psalms for their inspiration, and in doing so, have given us a great variety of settings, for different voices and instrumentations.

In compiling *More Than Psalms*, we have been able to draw on this rich heritage, selecting repertoire which we hope will be useful within the context of services and concerts. Here you will find music from the seventeenth to the twentieth centuries, from a wide range of composers, in many styles, suitable for different seasons and occasions, and scored for choirs of four to nine parts, both accompanied and unaccompanied.

I am grateful to my fellow choral advisers at Novello for their suggestions and input, and also to Elizabeth Robinson for her untiring work in overseeing the preparation of this volume.

Barry Rose
Somerset, June 2003

Notes on the music

Herbert Howells · Behold, O God our defender
Herbert Howells set these two verses from Psalm 84 for the coronation of Queen Elizabeth II in Westminster Abbey on 2 June 1953, when they were sung as an introit between the Presentation of the Holy Bible, and the Collect for Purity at the start of the Communion Service.

The broad flowing phrases made a grand effect with the large choral forces and full orchestra, and the later provision of an organ accompaniment ensured that the work made its way into the repertoire of many church and cathedral choirs. The composer's individual stamp is everywhere – whether in the declamatory opening, or in the more tender moments at 'for one day in thy courts'.

All choral singers have reason to be grateful to Howells, not just for his inspirational output, but also for his system of notation, leaving none of us in any doubt as to the exact length for which notes are to be sung.

Samuel Sebastian Wesley · Cast me not away from Thy presence
There is a story that Wesley had a broken arm when he wrote this piece; if that is so, it may explain the extraordinarily painful progressions at the words 'that the bones which Thou hast broken may rejoice'! Whatever the reason that prompted him to set these verses from the proper psalm for Ash Wednesday Evensong, it remains one of the finest and most enduring pieces of nineteenth century church music. It was written in 1848 whilst Wesley was at Leeds Parish Church and, although sometimes sung unaccompanied, it gains considerably from a supportive and suitably dramatic organ accompaniment.

The move into the major key (bar 40) brings the more positive text to life, though here the singers need to take care to observe the *più animato* marking, perhaps slowing slightly from bar 54 to 55.

In line with modern notation, the original note values have been halved for this edition.

Thomas Attwood · Enter not into judgment
Organist of St. Paul's Cathedral (London) from 1796 until his death in 1838, Thomas Attwood was a pupil of Mozart and, in later life, a close friend of Mendelssohn, who dedicated Three Preludes and Fugues (Opus 37) to him. Attwood wrote a considerable amount of music for the theatre, seventeen operas, songs and instrumental pieces, as well as anthems and settings of the Canticles for both St. Paul's and the Chapel Royal. These words

– used as one of the introductory Sentences at Evensong in the Book of Common Prayer – were probably set as an introit for a Lenten service in the Cathedral.

The music is direct and simple and there is a certain solemnity in the opening passage sung by unison voices, doubled by the organ, and then followed by a four-part harmonisation of the melody. The contrasting dynamics can be used to great effect, and the manual and pedal markings in the organ part will lend weight to the contrasts.

The original time signature is $\frac{2}{2}$ but we have removed alternate bar-lines and publish it here $\frac{4}{2}$.

Orlando Gibbons · The eyes of all wait upon Thee, O Lord
The last seven verses of Psalm 145, set by Gibbons as his first set of *Preces and Psalmes for Whitsunday at Evensonge*, and preserved in manuscripts in the British Museum, Durham Cathedral Library, Lambeth Palace and Peterhouse, Cambridge.

Born in Oxford, Orlando Gibbons received his early musical education in Cambridge as a chorister at King's College, and at the age of 21, was appointed organist to the Chapel Royal of King James I.

His music radiates warmth and memorable melodies and this psalm, set in antiphonal form between four upper voices and a five-part chorus, is both majestic and yet very personal.

It is published a minor 3rd higher than the original version and the suggested tempo and all dynamic markings are editorial. In performance, a better balance may be achieved in the verse-sections with a light tenor occasionally doubling the lower phrases of the two alto parts.

Arthur Hutchings · God is gone up with a merry noise
Better known as an academic and writer, including of an authoritative assessment of nineteenth century church music, Arthur Hutchings began his musical life as a schoolmaster and church organist, where the language of the psalms would have been very familiar to him.

This setting opens with verses from Psalm 47, one of the proper psalms for Ascensiontide, and its quasi-fanfare phrases neatly underline the text at 'and the Lord with the sound of the trumpet'. The recurring triple-time section takes words from Psalm 68, bringing an extra element of celebration, and at its second appearance, the composer has slightly altered the text, adding a suitably festive *Alleluia*, before returning to Psalm 47 for the final phrase.

Samuel Sebastian Wesley · I am thine, O save me

A beautiful musical miniature, first published in 1857 in the short-lived monthly magazine *The Musical Remembrancer*. It was later revised and the new version of 1870 was dedicated to Dr. Linnington Ash, of Elmtree House, Holsworthy, Devon, with whom Wesley had forged a friendship after being invited to open the new organ in the local parish church.

With its unusual five-part scoring featuring two separate tenor parts, the music deftly paints the text in the composer's inimitable style. The opening treble phrase is somewhat reminiscent of the rising notes in the first chorus of the larger *Ascribe unto the Lord*, written around the same time, whilst the accompaniment demonstrates the enormous span of Wesley's own hands (see bars 27-29).

The *Grave* and metronome markings are Wesley's own, and though the accompaniment was conceived for manuals alone, it benefits from the discreet use of pedals available on modern organs.

Jonathan Harvey · I love the Lord

Nearly thirty years after it was composed, it is difficult to imagine the electrifying effect this adventurous composition had on what was then a comparatively staid repertoire in the field of Anglican church music. It was written in 1976 whilst the composer was teaching at Southampton University, and was a direct result of hearing Martin Neary's choir sing the liturgy when he attended services in nearby Winchester Cathedral. The composer writes 'the profound impression they have made provided the inspiration for the music. A G-major chord sounding through most of the singing depicts the joyful love and irrepressible faith of a soul that clings to its Lord, despite its suffering and anguish'.

Both that irrepressibility and the anguish are graphically portrayed in this unique setting – one of the milestones of choral music in the latter part of the twentieth century.

Barry Rose · I will lift up mine eyes

Specially composed for Her Majesty Queen Elizabeth's Silver Jubilee Service in St. Paul's Cathedral, London on 7 June 1977, this is an extended Anglican chant setting to one of the best known psalm texts.

The musical style reflects the place in the service at which it was sung – just before the Archbishop of York read a passage from Micah, Chapter 4 – and was conceived with the reverberant acoustics of the cathedral in mind, especially the high treble Fs.

The alternate pairs of verses – 3-4 and 7-8 used smaller forces on that occasion, and suit a smaller group and gentler approach, to contrast with the fuller sounds in verses 1-2, 5-6 and the Gloria.

Grayston Ives · Jubilate (O be joyful in the Lord)

An adventurous and stylish setting of the Jubilate, written for Guildford Cathedral choir to sing at the opening service of the 1972 Mayfield (Sussex) Festival.

Now Informator Choristarum at Magdalen College, Oxford, Grayston Ives was then a tenor lay-clerk with the Guildford choir, and already a gifted composer, having studied with Richard Rodney Bennett.

The insistently rhythmic repetition of the opening words ('O be joyful') leads to carefree exultation, in which the taut choral rhythms are underpinned by the often florid organ accompaniment. The broad and spacious rising 7th at 'O go your way' later gives way to moments of calm vocal beauty when the same interval, both falling and rising, is featured in the legato setting of 'for the Lord is gracious'. Gradually the opening rhythmic impetus reappears, culminating in an ebullient Gloria, and the final declamatory Amen.

William H. Harris · Let my prayer

A delicate and atmospheric setting which beautifully paints the text – you can almost see the smoke from the incense rising, in the opening phrases for three-part trebles. Written for the Coronation in 1953 (see also Herbert Howells' *Behold, O God our defender*), Harris's music, sung as a gradual on that occasion, brought a brief moment of calm and peace to the noise and pageantry of this great occasion.

In performance it would be possible for the upper parts to be distributed more equally, with some light 1st altos singing the 3rd treble part.

Edward C. Bairstow · Lord, I call upon Thee

This setting appeared as the monthly musical supplement for *The Musical Times* of January 1917. Written in a time of war (see also *Lord, Thou hast been our refuge*) the text, drawn from three different and unrelated psalms, was almost certainly chosen to reflect the country's preoccupations and fears at that time. Bairstow had recently been appointed organist at York Minster, an appointment he held until 1946.

The four-part choral writing is more adventurous than much church music of that time, and shows a rare understanding of word painting, contrasting textures and subtle key changes. The delicate phrase for the trebles at 'Let my prayer be set forth in Thy sight' appears in two different keys, and is in stark contrast to the quasi-recitative for the tenors and basses at 'Mine enemies live and are mighty'. After the pleading sentiments of 'Forsake me not', calm reappears, leaving just the treble voices to have the last word, on a sustained high E flat.

In performance, this piece demands fluidity in

tempo, from both singers and organist. Careful study and observance of the composer's stress markings and indications of changes of speed will ensure the successful communication of the meaning of the text.

Bernard Rose · Lord, I have loved the habitation of thy house (Domine, dilexi)

Bernard Rose wrote *Lord, I have loved the habitation of thy house* in 1957, when he was about to move from Queen's College, Oxford, to become Informator Choristarum at Magdalen, a post he held with great distinction until his retirement in 1981.

The dedication was to E.L. Griffiths, then headmaster of Salisbury Cathedral School, where Rose, his brother Ronald, and his three sons, Graham, Gregory and Nigel, had all been cathedral choristers. *Domine dilexi …* is the school motto, so these verses from Psalm 26 were a natural choice as a text.

The music demonstrates the composer's life-long admiration for English sixteenth-century polyphony, whilst also using his own distinctive harmonic style, culminating in a triumphant ending.

Lennox Berkeley · The Lord is my shepherd

Probably the most widely known and best loved, Psalm 23 has been set many times, and for any composer there must be the challenge of painting the text in a new and accessible style.

In 1975, Lennox Berkeley met that challenge supremely with his setting, to a commission from the Very Reverend Walter Hussey, for the 1976 celebrations of the 900th anniversary of the foundation of Chichester Cathedral. The delicate and memorable opening treble solo has a gently moving accompaniment which immediately paints a picture of serene 'still waters', whilst the use of differing keys and tonalities in the choral parts that follow aptly paint the changing moods of the text. A feeling of complete musical and textual unity is achieved when a transposed reiteration of the opening theme and words reappears at the end, gracefully returning to the original key of G major.

In performance, the optimum speed is the metronome marking given by the composer (not always the case!) and choir directors may wish to find time for careful rehearsal of the unaccompanied section from bars 19 to 26, paying particular attention to the tuning of the alto and bass parts, and the dynamic markings for the tenors and basses at 'I will fear no evil' (bar 21). Although a miniature, this elegant setting stands proud amongst the best of twentieth-century church music.

Charles Villiers Stanford · The Lord is my shepherd

A master of melody, Stanford's lilting $\frac{6}{8}$ tempo immediately creates a pastoral effect, preparing the way for the choir's first quiet entry. Through a series of three-bar phrases, the music flows through different moods, with the dark 'Yea, though I walk through the valley of the shadow of death' giving way to reassurance and a return to the original theme at 'for Thou art with me'.

A vigorous recitative-like section is given to unison tenors and basses in the D minor setting of 'Thou shalt prepare a table before me against them that trouble me', and the opening mood of assurance returns as the trebles sing 'but Thy loving kindness and mercy' to one of Stanford's most charming melodies, now in D major.

Appointed organist of Trinity College, Cambridge in 1873, whilst still an undergraduate, Stanford became professor of music at the University fourteen years later, a post he held for nearly forty years. His music still retains a rightful place in the repertoire; it is the work of a consummate musical craftsman.

Edward C. Bairstow · Lord, Thou hast been our refuge

This extended setting of verses from Psalms 90, 102 and 144 was the result of a commission for the 1917 Festival of the Sons of the Clergy in St. Paul's Cathedral, and the accompaniment was originally scored for full orchestra. At a time when the country was at war, the choice of text seems amazingly apposite, not least with its ending at verse 15 of Psalm 90 – 'Comfort us again, now after the time that Thou hast plagued us; and for the years wherein we have suffered adversity.' With its deep chromaticisms that begin in a minor key, there is a mood of foreboding in the introduction, but that resolves into a quiet assurance as the choir enters with its unaccompanied 'Lord, Thou hast been our refuge'. Throughout the whole piece, Bairstow shows himself yet again to be a master of text-painting, whether it is in the eerily hushed phrases at 'Man is like a thing of nought: his time passeth away like a shadow', or the triumphal 'But Thou, O Lord, shalt endure for ever'.

The mood of unease returns again in the last organ interlude where the final chords in each bar seem to be searching for a peaceful resolution, and that comes in a final sustained Amen.

As with *Lord, I call upon Thee*, the many moods and subtle tempo changes need to be carefully observed for a successful performance, and all parts in the choir will find that the composer has been punctilious in his markings, especially in accented and stressed syllables.

Bryan Kelly · O be joyful in the Lord

A recent commission for the 2003 Salisbury Diocesan Choirs Festival, the text is taken from *Common Worship - Services and Prayers for the Church of England*.

Bryan Kelly's music immediately paints the celebratory text with its 'bell-like' motifs in the accompaniment, against which the choirs make their initial impact with unison singing, dividing into layered two-part writing, and later into four-part harmony. The differing moods of the various sections and the several key changes are usually set and linked by the organ part, and complete musical unity is achieved as the opening key and time signature return for the joyful Gloria with its effective and declamatory Amens. Although an extended setting, the vocal parts are not difficult to learn, and will make a useful addition to any choir's repertoire for festal occasions.

Edward Elgar · O hearken Thou

A reflective setting of verses from Psalm 5, written for the coronation of King George V in Westminster Abbey on 22 June 1911. As a contrast, in a service of great pomp, pageantry and celebratory music, Elgar perfectly caught the mood for that very personal moment at which the new King made his communion. The short and appropriately delicate introduction leads to the first choral entry, which, on that occasion, was sung by a semi-chorus – the larger forces of a massed choir joining in at bar 28. As with so much of Elgar's choral writing, the most important element of a successful performance will be the ebb and flow of music which, although written within the constraints of bar lines, needs the sense of *rubato*, much of which is carefully indicated by the composer himself, by means of tenuto markings.

Originally scored for full orchestra, it was also published later with the Latin text *Intende voci orationis meae*.

Barry Rose · O Lord our governor

As with Psalm 121, I wrote this for a specific occasion – as an opening item for a concert given in St. Albans Cathedral by three large choral societies. There was a limited amount of rehearsal time available in a programme which also included Berlioz's *Te Deum*. Richard Bourne, the conductor, was anxious that the new piece could be quickly learned, would be within the vocal range of smaller choirs and also suitable for accompaniment in performance on the piano or the organ.

Those of you who perform this piece will soon realise that differing moods and key changes are set by the accompaniment, and there are just the two awkward vocal spots which will repay careful rehearsal – bars 47-50, and the final affirmative choir entry on the word 'in' at bar 137 (where the treble line pays homage to Basil Harwood's hymn tune to *Let all the world*).

Elsewhere there is a musical nod to Vaughan Williams, Elgar, and a not very well hidden minor version of a well-known nursery-rhyme at the point where the tenors/basses take the part of the oxen.

Bernard Rose · O praise God in his holiness

Following a visit to Canada, Bernard Rose was commissioned to write this setting of Psalm 150 for Christ Church Cathedral, Victoria, British Columbia, to celebrate the dedication of the new cathedral organ in 1980.

Published here for the first time, the festive nature of the text and the occasion is immediately apparent in the organ accompaniment, with its joyfully pealing bell-like scale – a recurring motif, which later appears in other keys.

Rose's declamatory and well crafted choral writing also catches the mood of joy, graphically painting the tuning of strings in bars 44-5, and paying homage to Benjamin Britten's *Rejoice in the Lamb* in bars 39-42.

Elsewhere, in the colourful organ part, there is a quote from Stanford's well-known chant setting of Psalm 150 (bars 17-24).

John Blow · O pray for the peace of Jerusalem

Chorister of the Chapel Royal, choirmaster of St. Paul's Cathedral and organist of Westminster Abbey, John Blow is amongst the most influential of the post-Commonwealth church musicians, not least as teacher of the young Henry Purcell.

This delightful and tuneful short setting of the last four verses of Psalm 122 was published by Henry Playford in the early 1700s, and has a charming musical innocence. The accompaniment may have been conceived for strings, or harpsi-chord with basso continuo, and it is quite possible for the solo part to be sung by a tenor, though there are no historical precedents that suggest this. There is room for a certain amount of discreet ornamentation to the flowing lines of the solo, and especially in the repeat of bars 35-40.

Richard Hinde · O sing unto the Lord

All efforts to track down the details of the composer of this fine verse-anthem have so far failed. I have known it for over forty years and had always attributed it to Richard Hinde of Lichfield. But the music archives at Lichfield Cathedral list only a Henry Hinde (d.1641) who is recorded as the first organist of the cathedral.

I first heard it in Ely Cathedral in the late 1950s and it was that choir, under the direction of Arthur Wills, which later recorded it. Dr. Wills's description succinctly sums it up – '...vigour, brilliance and sheer inventiveness ...'

This performing edition is based on two manuscript copies in my possession, one in F sharp minor and the other in F minor – we have chosen to stay with the latter. The accompaniment might have been on viols or on the organ, and when we used to sing it in St. Albans, I would accompany the solos on the chamber organ, whilst my associate would accompany the choruses on the main organ – with discreet (probably un-scholarly!) use of the pedals.

The attractive and melodic verses are given to SSATB soloists, and there is memorable text-painting for both soloists and chorus – e.g. 'with trumpets and the sound of the cornet', and at 'let the sea roar'.

Samuel Sebastian Wesley · Praise the Lord, my soul

Here is one of the least known of S.S. Wesley's large-scale anthems, dating from the period when he was organist at Winchester Cathedral: 1849-65. It draws its text from four different morning psalms as appointed in the Book of Common Prayer – 103, 3, 5, and 4 – and ends with the well-known setting of *Lead me, Lord*, often used on its own as a short anthem.

Ambitiously scored for five soloists and choir, the organ part was written for the composer himself to play at the dedication of a 'Father' Willis organ in Holy Trinity Church, Winchester on 10 September 1861. The busy semiquaver passages in bars 101-107 would certainly have shown off both the instrument and the player, and we know that both soloists and chorus were drawn from the cathedral choir for that special occasion. A subsequent printed edition indicated that the semiquavers in the organ part could be omitted, and chords substituted in their place.

This practical performing edition succeeds the one originally published by Novello & Co (Anthem 59) and makes no apology for the suggested use of pedals beyond the range of the pedal-boards of many organs of that period. I have also shortened a few of the original note values (e.g. the first note of bars 54 and 73) at points where the singers usually breathe, and made suggestions as to where the full choir might re-enter, after the extended solo passages that end around bar 154 (the composer's original takes the solo parts as far as the beginning of bar 167).

It is a piece which demands great sensitivity from the singers in responding to the differing moods of the text, so beautifully set by Wesley, and will repay the rehearsal time needed to bring cohesion and commitment to the various solos and full sections.

The suggested speed and most dynamic markings are editorial.

Sidney Campbell · Sing we merrily unto God our strength

An energetically rhythmic setting of words from Psalm 81, written whilst the composer was organist at Canterbury Cathedral. The dedication is to Peter Hurford and the St. Albans Diocesan Choirs Festival 1962 – a special year in the life of the music at St. Albans, marking the rebuilding of the cathedral organ and its dedication on 18 November. It is not surprising, therefore, that Sidney Campbell's music – sung for the first time a week later – gives considerable prominence to the organ part, whilst also bearing in mind the varying standards of the many church choirs taking part, with vocal parts that are economically written, one part often doubling another. The whole effect is one of celebration and unrestrained joy.

Thomas Attwood · Turn Thee again, O Lord

Another short anthem, probably written for a special service at St. Paul's. The composer's markings assign different sections to groups titled semi-chorus, verse, and chorus, indicating the presence of more than one choir – desirable for special occasions, since contemporary accounts tell us that the St. Paul's choir then consisted of just eight boys and six men!

With its use of triple time, there is a charming musical innocence which lightens the weighty text in which the psalmist is imploring the Lord to be gracious unto his servants.

In my time at St. Paul's we sang this both unaccompanied (with the organ pedals, and/or the choir basses holding a low F from bar 52 to the end) and also with organ accompaniment throughout, and it is effective either way. The verse marking at bar 18 indicates a smaller group, though it could be sung by a competent solo quartet.

Barry Rose

Behold, O God our defender

Psalm 84, vv.9-10

Herbert Howells
(1892-1983)

4

6

rit.   al   meno mosso

più rit.   assai lento

Christmas Day, 1952

Cast me not away from Thy presence

Psalm 51, vv.11, 12, 17, 8

Samuel Sebastian Wesley
(1810-76)

The original is in $\frac{4}{2}$ time

12

16

Enter not into judgment

Psalm 143

Thomas Attwood
(1765-1838)

judg - ment with thy ser - vant, O Lord, for in thy sight shall no man

Ped.

liv - ing be jus - ti - fied, for in thy

liv - ing be jus - ti - fied, for in thy sight, for in thy

liv - ing be jus - ti - fied, for in thy sight, for in thy

liv - ing be jus - ti - fied, for in thy sight,

Man.

The eyes of all wait upon Thee, O Lord

Psalm 145, vv.15-21

Orlando Gibbons
(1583-1625)
ed. Barry Rose

From *Mr. Orlando Gibbons' Preces and Psalms for Whit-Sunday at Evensong.* Original in G.

22

24

26

(Ped.)

God is gone up with a merry noise

Psalms 47, vv.5-6;
68, v.18

Arthur Hutchings
(1906-89)

Very good choirs should sing this a tone higher.
The note values have been halved from the original (NOV 290311)

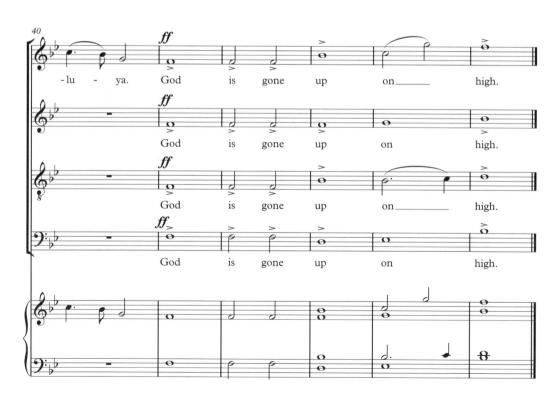

Dedicated to Dr. Linnington Ash

I am thine, O save me

Psalm 119, vv.94, 92

Samuel Sebastian Wesley
(1810-76)
ed. Watkins Shaw

* Editorial substitute for the lower manual compass of Wesley's organ, requiring

40

A Editorial tion. B Editorial adaptation for small hands. C — Wesley's organ part as in his earlier version of the anthem

In memoriam N.H.H.
for Martin Neary and the Choir of Winchester Cathedral

I love the Lord

Psalm 116, vv.1-4, 7-9

Jonathan Harvey
(b.1939)

44

48

52

lips closed

for HM The Queen's Silver Jubilee Service in St. Paul's Cathedral, 7th June 1977

I will lift up mine eyes

Psalm 121

Barry Rose
(b.1934)

6 So that the sun shall not burn thee. by   day:___   neither. the   moon   by   night.

(Ped.)

7 The Lord shall preserve thee from   all   evil: yea it is even he. that shall   keep   thy   soul:

mp

senza Ped.

8 The Lord shall preserve
thy going out and thy com - ing   in:___   from this time forth for   e - ver - more.

senza Ped.

Glory   be   to the   Father,   and to the Son, and. to the   Ho - ly   Ghost;

f

(Ped.)

As it was in the beginning, is now and. ever   shall   be: world without end.___   A -   men.

Ped.

Commissioned for the Mayfield Festival by the Mayfield Parish Chamber of Trade,
and first performed on 13 May 1972

Jubilate
O be joyful in the Lord

Psalm 100

Grayston Ives
(b.1948)

Man.

Gt.

Ped.

O be joy-ful in the Lord,___ in the

O be joy-ful___ in the Lord,___ in the

O be joy-ful in the Lord,___

O be joy-ful___ in the Lord,___

Gt. to Ped. off

be thank-ful___ un-to him, and speak good of his Name.

be thank-ful___ un-to him, and speak good of his Name.

be thank-ful un-to him,_____ and speak good of his Name.

be thank-ful un-to him,_____ and speak good of his Name.

64

Let my prayer

Psalm 141, v.2

William H. Harris
(1883-1973)

Lord, I call upon Thee

Psalms 141, vv.1, 2;
38, vv.19-22;
4, v.9

Edward C. Bairstow
(1874-1946)

80

to E.L. Griffiths Esq. J.P., and the Cathedral School of the Blessed Virgin Mary, Salisbury

Lord, I have loved the habitation of thy house
(DOMINE DILEXI)

Psalm 26, vv.8-12

Bernard Rose
(1916-96)

Written for the 900th anniversary of the foundation of Chichester Cathedral
and dedicated to the Very Rev. Walter Hussey, Dean of Chichester

The Lord is my shepherd
Op. 91, No.1

Psalm 23, vv.1, 2 & 4

Lennox Berkeley
(1903-89)

17

for his name's sake. Yea, though I

for his name's sake. Yea, though I

for his name's sake. Yea, though I walk through the val - ley

for his name's sake. Yea, though I walk through the val - ley

20

walk through the val - ley of the sha - dow of death,

walk through the val - ley of the sha - dow of death,

of the sha - dow of death, I will fear no e - vil,

of the sha - dow of death, I will fear no e - vil,

94

April 1975

The Lord is my shepherd

Psalm 23

Charles Villiers Stanford
(1852-1924)

114

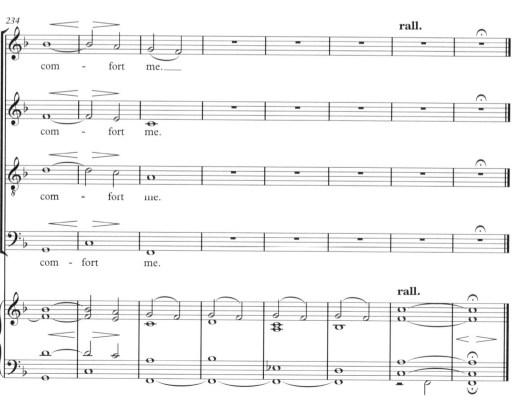

Lord, Thou hast been our refuge

Psalms 90, vv.1, 2 and 15;
144, vv.3, 4;
102, vv.12, 13

Edward C. Bairstow
(1874-1946)

from one ge - ne - ra - tion to a - no - ther.

from one ge - ne - ra - tion to a - no - ther.

from one ge - ne - ra - tion to a - no - ther.

from one_ ge - ne - ra - tion to a - no - ther.

Be - fore the

16′(Open)

Lord, what is man, that Thou hast such re-spect un-to him; or the

122

* If the 1st Sopranos sing the small notes, the Tenors must do the same in bar 133.

Commissioned by the Salisbury Diocesan Choral Festival Group
for the Joint Diocesan R.S.C.M. Festival 2003

O be joyful in the Lord

Psalm 100

Bryan Kelly
(b.1934)

144

O hearken Thou
Op. 64

Composed for the Coronation of King George V and Queen Mary (1911)

Psalm 5, vv.2, 3

Edward Elgar
(1857-1934)

for Richard Bourne, Stanmore Choral Society, Harrow Choral Society and Harrow Philharmonic Choir

O Lord our Governor

Psalm 8

Barry Rose
(b.1934)

156

160

161

-min - ion of the works of thy hands: *mp* and thou hast put
-min - ion of the works of thy hands: and thou hast put
-min - ion of the works of thy hands:
-min - ion of the works of thy hands: *mp* and thou hast put

rall. **a tempo** *mp*
All

all things in sub - jec - tion un - der his feet; All

mm

all things in sub - jec - tion un - der his feet; *mm*

Solo stop

Commissioned by Christ Church Cathedral, Victoria, B.C.
for the occasion of the replacing of the organ, 1980.

O praise God in his holiness

Psalm 150

Bernard Rose
(1916-96)

* A quotation from C.V. Stanford's chant to Psalm 150

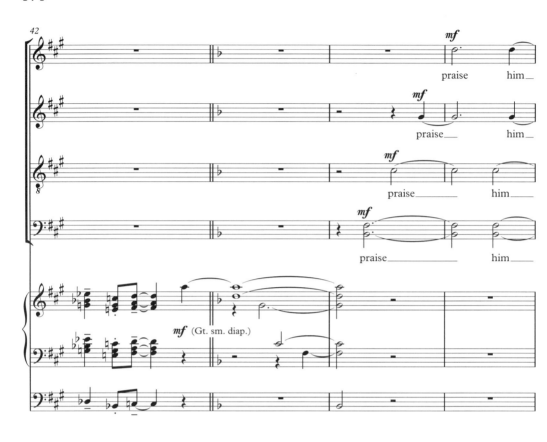

O pray for the peace of Jerusalem

Psalm 122, vv.6-9

John Blow
(1649-1708)
ed. Watkins Shaw

In this edition for practical use, the anthem has been transposed from the key of G, and in the triple time sections the crotchet has been treated as the customary unit. The organ part, together with marks of expression and speed, is the work of the editor, who is indebted to Mrs. E. K. Penn of Whiston Manor, Northants for drawing his attention to the early printed copy in Playford's "Divine Companion."

peace be with-in thy walls, peace, peace___ be with-in thy walls, and plen-teous-

-ness with-in thy pa - la - ces, and plen - teous-ness with-in thy pa - la-

For my breth-ren and com-pa-nions' sakes, I will wish thee pros-per - i-

-ty. Yea, be - cause of the house of the Lord our___ God, I will

seek, I will seek, I will seek to do thee good. I will good.

For my breth-ren and com-pa-nions' sakes, I will

* Here and in similar passages the original notation was ♩ ♪

O sing unto the Lord

Psalm 96

Richard Hinde
17th century
ed. Barry Rose

* optional

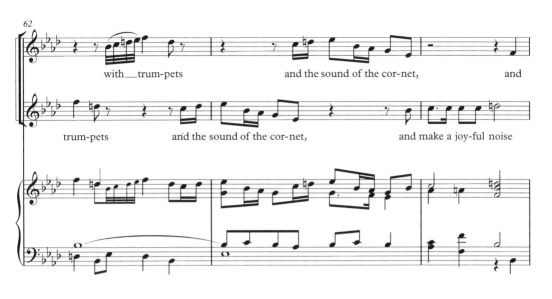

with _ trum-pets and the sound of the cor-net, and

trum-pets and the sound of the cor-net, and make a joy-ful noise

make a joy-ful noise un - to the Lord the King, With

un - to the Lord the King, un - to the _ Lord the King, With

With

With

With

Praise the Lord, my soul

Psalms 103, v.1;
3, v.5;
5, vv.1-3, 7-8, 12;
4, v.9

Samuel Sebastian Wesley
(1810-76)
Performing edition by Barry Rose

204

ear. Give ear,

O Lord, give ear un - to my

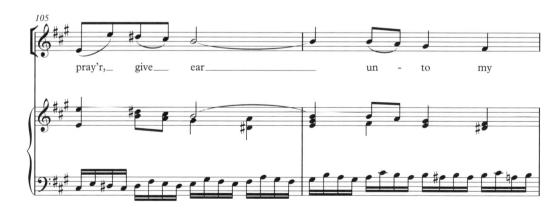

pray'r,__ give__ ear_____ un - to my

Ped.

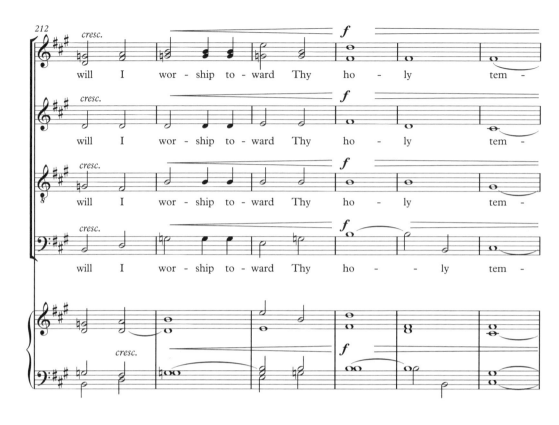

will I wor - ship to - ward Thy ho - ly tem -

will I wor - ship to - ward Thy ho - ly tem -

will I wor - ship to - ward Thy ho - ly tem -

will I wor - ship to - ward Thy ho - ly tem -

- ple.

- ple. Lead me, Lord, lead me in Thy right-eous-ness: make Thy way

- ple.

- ple.

Man.

for Peter Hurford and the St Albans Diocesan Choirs' Festival 1962

Sing we merrily unto God our strength

Psalm 81, vv.1-4

Sidney Campbell
(1909-74)

234

Turn Thee again, O Lord

Psalm 90, v.13

Thomas Attwood
(1765-1838)

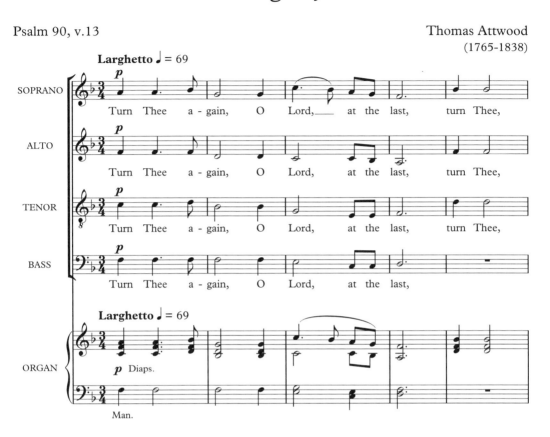

41

turn Thee, turn Thee, O Lord, at___ the last,___ and be gra - cious, be

turn Thee, turn Thee, O Lord, at the last, be

turn Thee, turn Thee, O Lord, at the last,___ and be gra - cious un - to Thy

O Lord, at the last, and be gra - cious un -

46

gra - cious un - to Thy ser - vants, un - to Thy ser - vants, be gra - cious, be

gra - cious un - to Thy ser - - - -

ser - - - - - vants, be gra - cious, be

- to Thy ser - - vants, be gra - cious, be

Sources of psalm texts used in this anthology